Margaret

ISBN 1-888045-18-3

Library of Congress Control Number: 2004103639

10 9 8 7 6 5 4 3 2 1

Typography and title lettering by Michael Manoogian
Typeset in Cantoria MT Light
Original illustration done in pencil and watercolor
Printed in Hong Kong by American Book

Action Publishing LLC
PO Box 391
Glendale, CA 91209

Visit us at actionpublishing.com

Margaret

written and illustrated by
Jeremy Dubow

Action Publishing

This is Margaret.

She lives here.

She brings the sun up

to make sure it's shining.

And plays with
the trees

to make sure they're
strong.

She frolics in the grass

to make sure it's soft.

And picks the flowers

to make sure they're pretty.

She splashes
      the birds
to make sure
      they can fly,

and to make sure the water's

wet.

She makes sure the wind's blowing

and then races the clouds.

She rolls down the hills
    to make sure they're still going down.

And catches her breath
to make sure she's standing still.

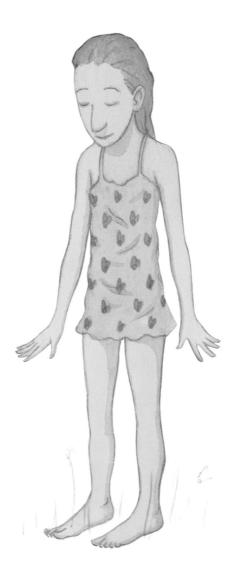

When the
day is over

she puts the sun to bed.

And says hello to the moon
and the stars to make sure
they're still there.

And then she goes to bed.